Big Panda, Little Panda

Scholastic Children's Books,
Scholastic Publications Ltd,
7-9 Pratt Street, London NW1 OAE, UK

Scholastic Inc.,
555 Broadway, New York, NY 10012, USA

Scholastic Canada Ltd,
123 Newkirk Road, Richmond Hill,
Ontario, Canada L4C 3G5

Ashton Scholastic Pty Ltd,
PO Box 579, Gosford, New South Wales,
Australia

Ashton Scholastic Ltd,
Private Bag 92801, Penrose, Auckland,
New Zealand

First published in hardback by Scholastic Publications Ltd, 1993
This edition published 1994

Text copyright © Joan Stimson, 1993
Illustration copyright © Meg Rutherford, 1993

ISBN: 0 590 55423 9

Printed in Hong Kong by the Paramount Printing Group.

Big Panda, Little Panda

Joan Stimson

Illustrated by
Meg Rutherford

Hippo

Ever since the little panda
could remember, he'd been
called Little Panda.

When he was tiny, his mother
fed him many times a day.
"Who's the best-looking
Little Panda in the whole
wide world?" she whispered
and held him close.

When Little Panda began to pad about, he often fell and hurt himself. But Mum was always there to scoop him up. "There, there, Little Panda. What a nasty bump."

And every night, when she tucked him in, his mother sang a lullaby. Then, when he was not quite such a little panda, she began to read to him from the old storybook.

One night Mum held Little Panda extra
close. "Who's the best-looking
Big Panda?" she whispered.

Little Panda was puzzled. He looked
around the room and shook his head.
Then his mother explained.
"Very soon there will be a new Little
Panda and I shall need a great Big
Panda to help look after us."

The new Little Panda arrived even
sooner than expected.

And in no time at all the new Big Panda
was rushed off his paws.

He hurried and fetched.
He scurried and carried.
Big Panda worked so hard
that he was almost
always hungry.

"Can I have something to
eat?" asked Big Panda
ten times a day.
But his mother didn't
always hear him. She was
too busy feeding Little Panda and
whispering, "Who's the prettiest Little
Panda in the whole wide world?"

One day Big Panda was rushing
so fast that he fell down hard.
"O U C H !"
Big Panda clambered
onto Mum's knee
and showed her
his paws.

Mum looked up.
But not for long.
"Never mind, Big
Panda. It's only a
little scratch."

After supper Big Panda found
the old storybook.
"Will you read to me?"
he asked.

But, before they could begin, Little Panda
started to cry.
"I won't be a minute," said Mum.

When at last she came back, Mum gave a
huge yawn. She began to turn the pages
of the storybook faster and faster.

"Stop!" cried Big Panda.
"You're missing out
the best bit."

But he was too late.
Mum was already
snoring.

Big Panda was fed up!
Fed up with fetching.
Fed up with carrying.
Fed up with waiting for
food and stories.
Fed up because nothing
was fun any more.
"I don't like being big,"
he sniffed.

So Big Panda wrapped
Little Panda in a blanket
and tucked her in *his* bed.
Then he padded back to
Little Panda's bed and
squeezed in.

When at last she woke up, Mum looked for
a long time at the two pandas.
She remembered the unfinished story.
"I'm sorry, Big Panda," she whispered.

Next morning Mum was up early. And so
was Little Panda.
"Where are you going?" cried Big Panda.
"Come on, we're going out," said Mum.
"We all need a change."

Mum led the way to the forest.
All day long the pandas played.
They slid down banks and climbed trees.
They chased butterflies and found an echo.

That night Mum was
exhausted. But she still
had a story to finish.
"Where are you, Big
Panda?" she called.

At first there was no reply.
Then suddenly a huge furry ball crashed
into view. The pandas' home shuddered.
"Good heavens!" cried Mum.
"Whatever's that?"
The furry ball gurgled and giggled.

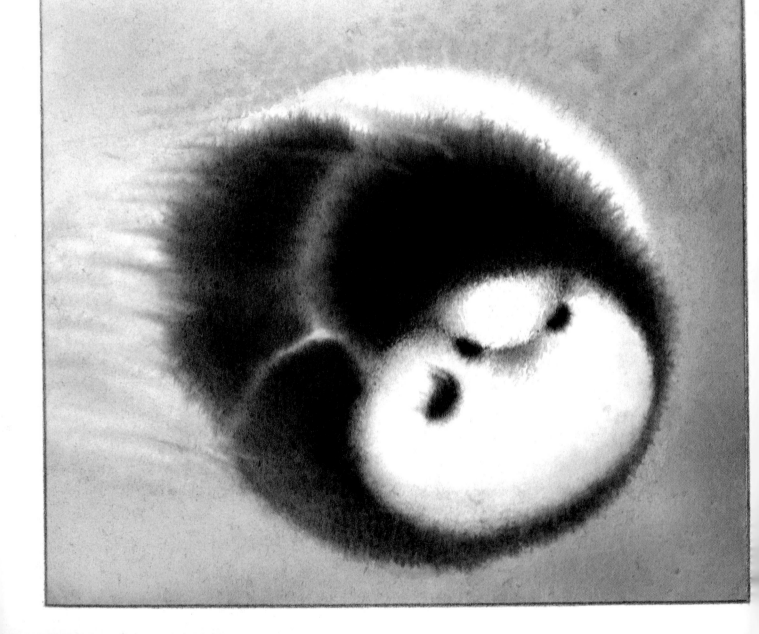

It's Little Panda and meee!" came the reply.
And before she knew it Mum was part of
the game.

Mum picked herself up.
She tried to get on with
the story. But Big Panda
kept interrupting.

"Look at us, look at us," he cried.
"I'm teaching Little Panda to stand
on her head."

At last the pandas ran out of puff and Mum
began to read.
"Oh dear," she yawned. "I can hardly keep
my eyes open."
"Never mind," cried Big Panda. He reached
across for the book. "I can read the story
tonight. Because I really am
Big Panda now...

And I think I'm going to like
being *big* after all."

Sometimes you want to stay little
even though you're big.

When Little Panda gets a baby sister, he's not at all
sure he likes it. Suddenly Little Panda has become
BIG PANDA. What's more, Mum doesn't even have
time to read him his story – she's so tired she falls
asleep halfway through...

A story for all children coming to terms with the
arrival of a baby sister or brother.

"a charming, gentle story" – *The Independent*

ISBN 0-590-55423-9

UK **£3.99**

SCHOLASTIC

9 780590 554237 >